THE SLEEPING SWORD

MICHAEL MORPURGO

ILLUSTRATED BY MICHAEL FOREMAN

To the people of Bryher,
for all the warmth and kindness
over the years.
M.M.

First published in Great Britain 2002
by Egmont Books Limited
239 Kensington High Street, London W8 6SA

ISBN 0 7497 4852 4

10 9 8 7 6 5 4 3 2 1

A CIP catalogue record for this title is available from the British Library

Typeset by Dorchester Typesetting Group Ltd

Printed and bound in Great Britain by Bath Press Ltd, Somerset

CONTENTS

Before I wrote my story 1

The Sleeping Sword by Bun Bendle

1 The dive of my life 5
2 'Not a mummy mummy' 11
3 Inside my black hole 15
4 Only one way out 19
5 Hell Bay 25
6 One of us 31
7 'Be Happy. Don't worry.' 37
8 'Be an angel, Bun' 45
9 Dry bones 49
10 'Isn't that magical?' 57
11 'No such thing as luck' 63
12 In my dreams 71
13 The quest begins 77
14 Ghost ship 81
15 Metamorphosis 85
16 Arthur, High King of Britain 89
17 The sleeping sword 93
18 End of the quest 101
19 'Is it really true?' 109

After I wrote my story 114

The Isles of Scilly

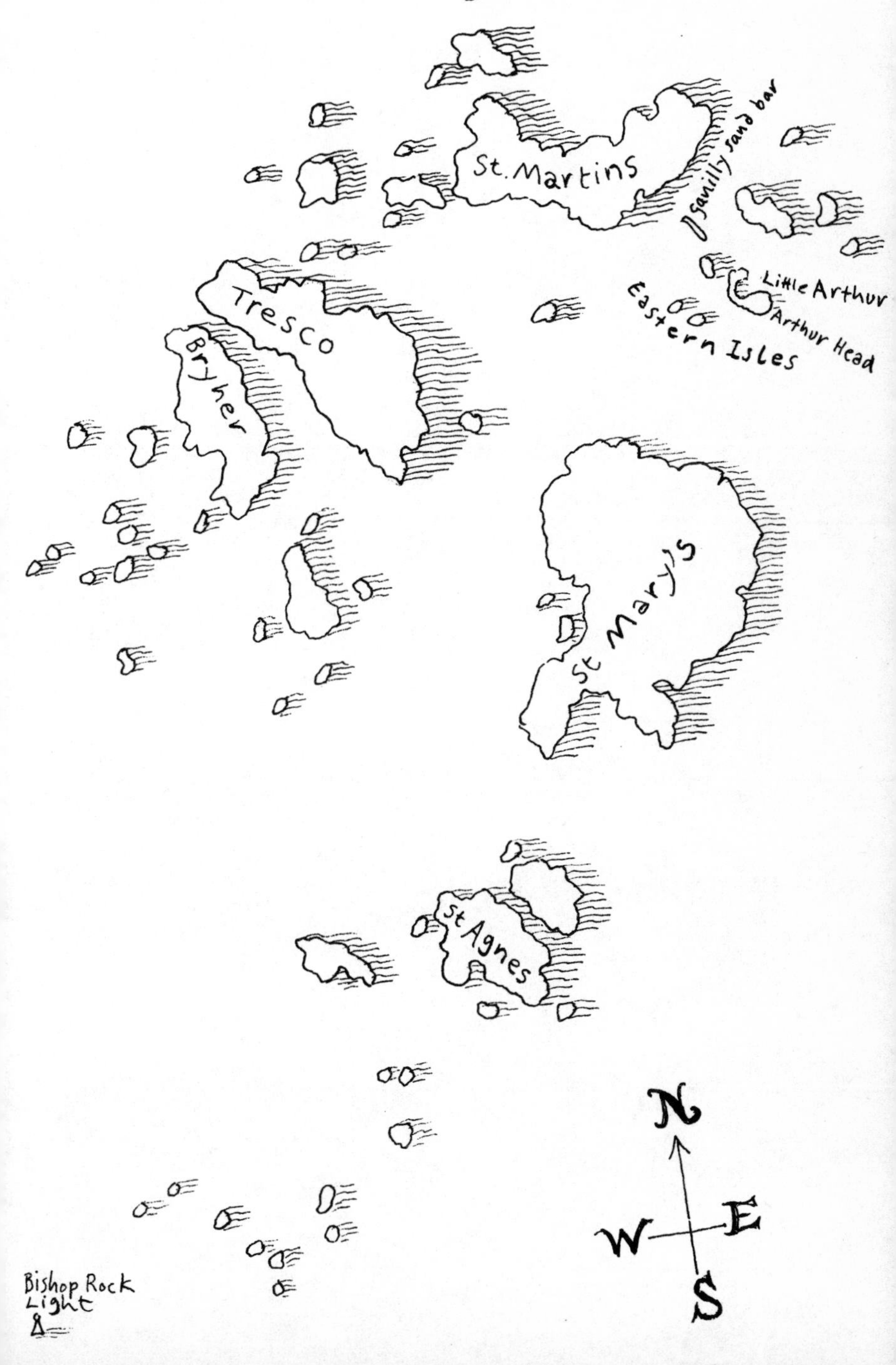

BEFORE I WROTE MY STORY

Before it happened, before the world went black about me, I used to read a lot. I've tried Braille, and I am getting better at it all the time, but reading is so slow that way. So now I listen to my audio tapes instead. I've got dozens of them on my shelf. The trouble is I can't tell which is which, so I've put my three favourite ones side by side on my bedside table. That way I can find them more easily.

Left to right, it's *The Sword in the Stone, Sir Gawain and the Green Knight,* and *Arthur, High King of Britain*. I've listened to those three so often I can say bits of them by heart. But it's *Arthur, High King of Britain* I've listened to most often, not because it's the best – *The Sword in the Stone* is probably the best – but because *Arthur, High King of Britain* begins and ends on Bryher, on the Scilly Isles, where I live. I can picture all the places so well inside my head and that helps me to feel part of the story, free to roam inside it somehow, to be whoever I want to be, do whatever I want to do.

And that's my trouble at the moment. There's so

much I can't do now that I used to do without even thinking about it – you know, ordinary things like going down to the shop, hurdling over mooring ropes, playing football on the green, watching telly, seeing my friends whenever I felt like it, messing about in boats, diving off the quay with them in the summertime. I can still go swimming, but someone always has to be with me. That's the worst of it, really. I can never go free like I used to.

It's not so bad at home. I've got a sort of memory-and-touch map of the house inside my head, every room, every doorway, every chair. And, provided my father doesn't leave his slippers in the middle of the kitchen floor – which he often does – and provided no one shifts the furniture or moves my toothbrush, I can manage just about all right. I really hate it if I trip or fumble about or fall over. No one laughs, of course they don't. In a kind of way I wish they would. Instead they go all silent and feel sorry for me, and that just makes me angry again inside.

And there's so much I miss – all the colours of the sky and the sea, the blue and the green and the grey, the black and white of the oystercatchers. I can't picture colours in my head any more, and I can't picture people's faces either, not like I could. So, like the oystercatchers, everyone's a voice now, just a voice. I'm getting used to it, or that's what I keep telling myself, anyway. I should be after two years. But it still makes me angry when I think about it, the bad luck of it, I mean. I try not to think about it, but that's a lot easier said than done.

That's what's so good about 'reading' stories, and 'writing' them, too. I've made up lots and lots of short stories. I love doing it because I can be whoever I like inside my stories. I can make my dreams really happen. I'm the maker of new worlds. Inside my dreams, inside my stories I can run free again. I can see again. I can be me again.

I don't actually write my stories, not like other people do. I find the Braille machine slows me down, like it does with my reading. Instead, I tell them out loud into a recorder. That's how I'm doing this now, and it's brilliant, because it lets the story flow. I get things wrong of course, and often too, but I just record over my mistakes and on I go. Easy.

A few days ago, I finished my very first long story and this is it. It took me the whole of the summer to write it. It's dedicated to Anna – you'll see why soon enough – and I've called it . . .

THE SLEEPING SWORD

BY BUN BENDLE

For Anna

CHAPTER 1

THE DIVE OF MY LIFE

IT WAS NO ONE'S FAULT EXCEPT MINE. I WAS showing off. True, I didn't exactly want to go in the first place, but then I shouldn't have allowed Liam and Dan to persuade me. On the way back on the school boat from Tresco it had been cold and blustery. All I wanted to do was to get back home and finish reading my book about King Arthur.

Mum was out somewhere on the farm when I got in. We grow organic vegetables (onions, courgettes, tomatoes, lettuces – all sorts) to sell to the visitors – we get a lot of tourists on Bryher, especially in the summer. As usual, she had left my tea on the table. Dad was out checking his lobster pots. I was deep in my book, munching away at my peanut butter sandwich, when Liam and Dan banged on the window. They were in their wetsuits and breathless with running.

'Bun, we're going down the quay,' Liam shouted. 'You coming?' It wasn't really a question at all.

'I'm reading,' I replied, 'and, anyway, it's cold.' Liam ignored me.

'See you down there,' he said, and they were gone.

On Bryher we were the only boys of about the same age (there's only eighty people living here on the island anyway; one shop, one church, no school). We grew up together, went over to Tresco school every day together, we went fishing together, did just about everything together. 'The Three Musketeers' they call us. If we had a leader it was Liam, most of the time, anyway. He was the smallest of the three of us, and was by far and away the cleverest, too. He had a real gift of the gab, and was a fantastic mimic, as well. Anyone from Mrs Gee ('BF' Gee we called her) in the shop – 'Get your mucky hands off my ice-creams' – to 'Barking' Barker our head teacher – 'Look at my voice, Liam, I'm speaking to you!'

Dan was like a big friendly puppy, full of energy and bouncy. He always made us laugh a lot. Of the three of us I was the quietest, happy enough usually to go along with whatever the other two dreamed up. I just liked being with them. But I had my own very private reason, too, for going along with them. Anna.

Anna was Dan's big sister, and I loved her. Simple as that. I loved her. I couldn't tell her of course, because I was ten and she was fourteen. I didn't love her just because she was beautiful, which she was (just the opposite in every way to big, lumpy Dan), but also because we talked – and I mean *really* talked – about things that really mattered, like books, like feelings, like oystercatchers. Liam and Dan were my mates, best mates, but Anna was my best friend and had been as long as I could remember.

I was finding it difficult to concentrate on my book. I kept regretting I hadn't gone with them down to the quay. It was the sudden thought that it was Friday and that Anna might possibly be there, back for the weekend from secondary school on St Mary's, that finally decided me. I would finish the book later.

I pulled on my wetsuit and ran down the sandy track through the farm to the quay. As I rounded the corner by the shed, I saw them all larking about on the quay. Anna *was* there. She'd already been in swimming, I could see that, but the other two hadn't. They were standing on the edge, looking down into the water and hesitating.

The sea was murky and choppy and uninviting. I didn't want to go in, not one bit, but Anna had seen me. I saw an opportunity to impress her, and just went for it. I charged down the quay going full pelt, screaming like a mad thing. Anna tried to wave me down but I ignored her.

I dodged past Dan, who was shouting at me to stop, sprang off and launched myself into the most spectacular swallow dive I could, the best dive of my life, just for her. I remember thinking that it seemed to be taking longer than it should to reach the water. After that I remember nothing.

CHAPTER 2

'NOT A MUMMY MUMMY'

WHEN I CAME TO, I KNEW AT ONCE I WAS IN hospital. Nowhere else sounds or smells like a hospital. At first I thought that I was back visiting Gran in hospital in Truro, but then I realised that it was me lying there on a bed, not Gran. I couldn't see where I was because there was a bandage round my eyes. I could feel it. In fact, most of my head seemed to be swathed in bandages. Someone was holding my hand and telling me not to worry, not to move. It was my mother. I wasn't worried, but I was hurting. My whole head was heavy with pain.

'What happened?' I asked.

'You're fine, Bundle. You're in hospital. You had an

accident.'

'What happened?' I asked again.

'You went in off the quay. But the water was too low. Your head hit a stone. You were lucky, Bundle. It could have been a lot worse.' It felt bad enough to me.

'You need water to dive into, Bun, you silly chump. Didn't you know that?' My father was there too, and his voice sounded strange, as if he'd been crying. Now I *was* worried. 'Created quite a stir, you did,' he went on. 'Anna dragged you out of the sea, and gave you mouth-to-mouth. You'd have drowned else, and the boys went for help. We had the air ambulance in and they flew us straight here to Truro.'

'You've broken your arm, and you've had a bit of an operation on your head,' my mother was saying, 'so you'll have to stay in here for a few days. You sleep now.'

She didn't have to tell me. I was already drifting away. I was in and out of sleep for days and nights, nearly a week they told me afterwards. My mother always seemed to be there when I woke up. Doctors and nurses came, to ask questions mostly and occasionally to examine my head. These were the only times the bandage came off – not that it made any difference, because my whole face was still so swollen that I couldn't even open my eyes to see.

The doctors always seemed very pleased with me. I was making a good recovery. I wasn't to worry they said. The swelling would go down in time and I'd be going home soon. I had visitors every day and my mother would always tell them the same thing, that I had had a very lucky escape, that I'd be fine.

I woke up one afternoon and heard my mother saying much the same thing, again. 'He'll be fine. But if it hadn't been for you, Anna, there'd have been no lucky escape at all, and that's the truth of it.' Anna was there! In the room! She'd come to visit me. Oh God, how I wished I could see her.

'And you two boys,' my mother went on, sounding a bit weepy - it could only be Liam and Dan - 'going for help like you did. You were wonderful, all of you, truly wonderful.'

I didn't know what to say to any of them. I was overjoyed they were there, but somehow I couldn't say it. Why is it that the most important things are so difficult to say? As it was I just pretended I was asleep under my bandages, and listened.

'He's sleeping now,' my mother was saying. 'But the doctors are sure he'll be fine. Like I said, he's lucky to be alive. You stay with him for a while, will you? I need to see the staff nurse. I shan't be a moment.' And I heard her go out.

For some moments no one spoke. Then Dan whispered, 'With all those bandages, he looks like a mummy or something. Not a mummy mummy – an Egyptian tomb mummy, the haunting kind. You know what I mean.' At that, I curled my hands into claws and then rose up, howling horribly. The giggling that followed was infectious. In the end all four of us were quite helpless with it. It made my head hurt, but I didn't mind. I was just so happy, so relieved to be back with them.

'I'll come and see you again, Bun,' Anna said as she left. 'As often as I can.'

I cried behind my bandages when they left, but out of joy, not sadness. Anna had come to see me, and she'd be back. I'd be out of hospital and home in just a week, a couple at the most, that's what they'd told me. Everything would be back to normal.

CHAPTER 3

INSIDE MY BLACK HOLE

THE NEXT DAY THE BANDAGES CAME OFF SO that the doctor could examine the wound on the side of my head. 'Good, Bun, very good,' said the doctor. 'The swelling's gone right down. You can open your eyes now.'

It took some doing – they felt a bit gummed up. But I did it. I opened them. The trouble was that I couldn't see anything. I blinked and tried again. Blackness. Only blackness. I squeezed them tight shut, and opened them again. I felt I was deep inside a black hole, that there was no way out. I was drowning in blackness, unable to breathe, my heart pounding with sudden terror.

'That looks a lot better, Bun,' the doctor went on, turning my head with his cold hands, 'a lot better.'

'I can't see,' I told him. 'I can't see.' There was a long silence. Then I could feel his breath on me, his face close to mine. He was lifting my eyelids.

'What about now?' he asked me. 'Can you see a light? Can you see anything?'

'No,' I said.

'What's the matter with him, Doctor?' My mother was asking just the question I wanted to ask, and she was frightened, really frightened. I could hear it in her voice.

'Well, it's a little difficult to say at this stage,' the doctor said. 'I expect it's just a side effect of the trauma. He's had a nasty crack on his head. It'll correct itself in time, I'm sure. But we'll do some tests. It's nothing to worry about, Bun.' His hand squeezed my shoulder. 'You'll be fine.'

If I had a pound for every time doctors told me that in the next few months, I'd be rich, extremely rich. But you can't blame them. What else could they say? They had to try to reassure me. Everyone was trying to reassure me. When they discharged me and I got back home, it was the same old refrain: 'Don't worry, Bun. It'll be fine.'

To begin with I believed them, because I wanted to believe them, needed to believe them. All the tests - and there were dozens and dozens of them, in Truro, in Bristol, in London - showed that I should be able to see. But the fact was that I couldn't.

Every morning I opened my eyes hoping and praying, but no longer believing, that this time I'd be able to see something. I never could. Everything else had healed up long ago by now. The plaster was off my broken arm, and the stitches out of my head.

Dan said cheerily, that he preferred me when I'd looked like a mummy. Liam, I could feel, didn't know what to say, so he said very little. He didn't know how to include me, so he didn't.

Only Anna didn't pretend with me, didn't feel awkward. She was just herself. She'd sit and talk, talk about anything and everything. She seemed to understand, without my having to tell her, what no one else did: that I felt lost, bewildered and frightened in a strange black world where I was entirely alone. She knew that I just wanted everyone to be normal, as they had been, so that I could still be part of the real world I remembered, their world.

My father was endlessly encouraging, taking me out on the fishing boat as he used to, trying to pretend my blindness didn't exist. From time to time I'd hear my mother crying quietly downstairs, and I knew only too well why. But when she was with me she was always positive, always concerned and comforting and cuddly, more so than she ever had been, too much so.

No one ever spoke the word 'blind', not in my hearing anyway, either at home or in the various hospitals. So in the end I mentioned it myself, to Anna, because I knew she'd be honest with me. 'I'm blind, aren't I?' I said to her, interrupting a story she was reading me.

'Yes,' she replied quietly. 'But because you're blind now, it doesn't mean you will be for ever, does it? I mean, your arm got better, so did your head. Why not your eyes?'

'What if I stay blind?' I asked her. 'What if I don't get better?'

'It won't change anything, not really. You'll still be the same person. I'll still be your friend. I always will be.' I cried then as I'd never cried before, and Anna put her arm round me. It wasn't exactly worth going blind to have her do that, but it comforted me as nothing else had; calmed my fears, made me feel less alone inside my black hole of despair.

CHAPTER 4

ONLY ONE WAY OUT

AFTER THAT, RESIGNATION GREW IN ME SLOWLY, imperceptibly. I would never see again. Never. There was to be no going back. I was going to have to live with myself as I was, sightless and alone, in permanent unending darkness. For a while I could think of nothing else and sank into a deep sadness, a bottomless pit of bitterness and self-pity. Anna tried to get me out of it, not by pitying me but by arguing with me.

'It's like a living death,' I told her once.

'You can't say that,' she said. 'You know nothing about death. You haven't been there and neither have I. We're alive. All right, so you can't see. But you can live. We've got to think about living.'

Anna came over to see me whenever she could, whenever she was home from school. More than anyone else she lightened my darkness. We'd talk of all the good times we'd had together and laugh about them. She brought me some of her CDs – Robbie Williams, Britney Spears, the Corrs – and some audio tapes as well – *The Sword in the Stone, Sir Gawain and the Green Knight*, and *Arthur, High King of Britain.* With their help I managed to banish the hateful silence of my room and to fill my life with sound. This seemed to help, to distract me, to take myself out of myself – at least, for a while. But as time went on I found I also had something else to worry about. I had tried to ignore it, to pretend it wasn't so. But I couldn't, not any longer.

At first I hoped it might be temporary, just a phase that would pass. But it didn't pass. If anything it became worse. It was something I had to hide, something I'd told no one about, not even Anna. Ever since the accident I had been unable to remember things, little things that might not have mattered so much on their own. But there were also, I discovered, important parts of my life that had just gone missing. For instance, apparently we'd all been on holiday to Canada when I was five, to see my uncle Bill, my father's brother, who lived in Toronto. People still talked about it. I remember I'd seen the photographs. It was the only time I'd been up in a jumbo jet. But I couldn't remember any of it.

Nor could I recall anything of a trip up to London only a year or so ago, when we'd been to the zoo, and to the Science Museum, to the Tower of London, and to Stamford Bridge to see my favourite team Chelsea playing Tottenham Hotspur. All these events were a complete mystery to me. In fact, I had no memories of even *being* a Chelsea fan.

My mind, I was discovering, was full of blank spaces, gaps in my memory that were completely unpredictable, so that I was never prepared for them.

The vicar came to see me one day – 'just to cheer you up,' as he put it – and started going on about a production of *Joseph and the Amazing Technicolor Dreamcoat* he'd put on the year before in the church, apparently.

'You've a fine singing voice, Bun,' he said. 'Everyone said so. You were a wonderful Pharaoh, just wonderful.'

I didn't have a clue what he was talking about. I had no memory of it whatsoever. I covered up as best I could, but how well I had covered up I could never really be sure, because of course I couldn't see people's faces to see how they reacted.

As each new memory gap became evident I became more and more terrified, because it made me fear I might now be losing my mind as well as my sight. It was my darkest, deepest secret and I kept it to myself.

There was even worse to come. It was becoming obvious that I couldn't go back to school with the others on Tresco, that sooner or later I'd have to go to a 'special' school for the blind. There was no school for the blind on Scilly. I'd have to go to the mainland. I'd have to leave home.

When the time came my mother tried to break it to me as gently as she could. 'All the kids have to go to school on the mainland at sixteen anyway, for their sixth form. You know that, Bundle. You'd just be doing the same thing, only a few years earlier, that's all. And it's just the right place for you. Dad and I have been to see it. They've got all the right equipment, all the specialist teachers you need. Lovely grounds, too. It's only up at Exeter. Not far. We can come and see you, and you can come back home often. I promise.'

It was the final confirmation that I was indeed different from everyone around me and that, therefore, I was to be treated differently.

'It won't be until the end of the summer, Bun,' said my father, laying a hand on my arm. 'And it won't be so bad, honest it won't. You'll see. I went away to school at your age, and I loved it. Lots to do, lots of new friends.'

I was to be separated from home, from everyone I knew and loved, my mother, my father, from Liam and Dan, and from Anna, too. It was more than I could bear. I lay there all night thinking it through. By the time I heard the dawn chorus of gulls and oystercatchers, I had made up my mind.

There was only one way out, and I would have to take it.

CHAPTER 5

HELL BAY

NOW THAT I'D MADE UP MY MIND I DIDN'T think twice about it. Still in my pyjamas, I picked up the boathook from the porch and walked out of the house, down the path to the front gate, and out on to the track. I hadn't been further than this on my own since the accident, and I knew that even with my boathook feeling the way for me, I'd be bound to stumble. The track up to Hell Bay was uneven and stony, difficult enough to climb *with eyes*, let alone without them. But I'd done it a thousand times before and I knew the lie of the land almost instinctively. I could do it.

I felt the hill rising under my feet as I came up to

Hillside Farm, where Anna lived, where she would be sleeping. I stopped for a few moments outside her house. 'Goodbye, Anna,' I whispered. 'Thanks for trying. Thanks for everything. I'm sorry.' I felt the tears coming, felt myself weakening.

I turned away and walked on, out around Bryher Pool and Popplestones Bay. Here I tripped and fell badly, barking my knee on the ground. I sat there for a while rocking back and forth, waiting for the pain to subside.

I heard a flock of turnstones peeping along the shore, and listened to the surge of the sea as each wave fell and washed up the beach. I knew that it was a beautiful world I was leaving, but it was a world I could no longer see, a world I no longer felt I belonged in.

As I got to my feet I thought I heard someone close behind me. I stood and listened for a while and decided I must have been imagining things. It must have been the wind sighing through the dunes. It was far too early for anyone to be about.

From now on the track was both steep and dangerous, easy enough to follow but narrow and tortuous, in places soft with springy thrift, then suddenly treacherous with loose stones underfoot and slippery wet rock. In places I had to go down on my hands and knees to feel my way forward.

When I came up over the crest of the hill overlooking Hell Bay, the sudden force of the wind took my breath away and chilled me to the bone. I could hear the roaring thunder of the sea. I could feel the whole island tremble under my feet as each wave pounded against the cliffs. I knew exactly where I was, exactly the place I would do it. It wasn't far now. I was almost there. I moved on unthinking, unfeeling, as if in a trance, as if led by some unseen hand towards the edge of the cliff, towards the end of my life.

A voice spoke from behind me, gentle, ethereal. 'Don't, Bun. Don't.' Then a hand, a real hand, grasped me firmly by the arm. It was Anna. 'Come away,' she said. 'Come away. You're too close to the edge.'

I did not resist as she led me away, her arm round me. She helped me down on to a carpet of soft thrift and sat down beside me, letting me cry until I had no more tears left to cry. She did not talk and she did not touch me, but I could feel her willing me to explain why I had tried to do it. She wanted to understand, she needed to.

So I told her why. I poured it all out about the 'special' school for the blind on the mainland, how they were banishing me to another world, forcing me away, driving me out. I had nothing to live for any more.

'Didn't you tell them? Didn't you tell them how you feel about it?' Anna asked me.

'Yes. Well, no. Not exactly. I tried, but I can't talk to them like I can to you. And maybe they're right, in a way. I am different now. Maybe there is no choice. Maybe I have to go. You won't tell them, will you? About this, I mean.'

'Course not, Bun. But if you won't tell them what you feel, then I will. We all will: Liam, Dan and me. We'll tell them we don't want you to go, that there's got to be another way. But you've got to promise me something. You've got to promise me, Bun, that you'll never give up, that you'll never think of killing yourself again. Promise?'

I promised, and I meant it. A promise to Anna was one I would always keep.

We started off back home, her hand holding mine tight all the way.

CHAPTER 6

ONE OF US

SOMETHING HAD BEEN PUZZLING ME BUT IT WAS only as we passed Anna's house that it came to me what it was.

'How did you know?' I asked her, 'I mean, how did you find me?'

'It was strange, really strange. I don't normally wake up this early. Something woke me. Like a voice in my head, part of a dream, maybe. I don't know. I was just about to go back to sleep when I heard footsteps outside. I opened the window and there you were walking away up the track in your pyjamas. I thought you were sleepwalking. I didn't know what else you could be doing. What I did know is that you're not supposed to wake up sleepwalkers, so I just followed you. But by the time you got to Hell Bay I knew you couldn't be sleepwalking. You seemed to know exactly where you were going. I never thought you were going to . . . you know . . . until the very last moment when you went near the edge.'

'I'm glad you woke me up,' I said.

'Me too,' she said, and she squeezed my hand. 'I'll talk to the others. We'll sort something. Don't worry.'

She took me as far as my front door and then left me. I found my way in all right and managed to get myself back upstairs and into bed without waking anyone up. I was exhausted, and went to sleep almost at once. When my mother woke me later, it was as if the whole thing had been some half-forgotten night-long dream. But my bruised knee and my gritty feet were real enough to convince me that some of it, at least, had been no dream.

Only when Anna and Dan and Liam turned up at the house that evening, and Anna began talking, could I be quite sure that I had dreamed none of it, none of it at all. Now I knew for certain that last night, up on the cliffs at Hell Bay, Anna had indeed saved my life – again.

'We've been talking, all of us,' Anna began

hesitantly, 'and we've been thinking, and . . . well, Bun says you want to send him off to a sort of special school on the mainland. And we . . .'

'No, Anna,' my mother interrupted. 'That's not right, and it's not fair. That's not how it is at all. We don't *want* to send Bun anywhere. Of course we don't, but we have to. He can't go back to school on Tresco. It wouldn't be fair on the teachers, or fair on Bun. They just couldn't cope. He needs to be taught by specialist teachers now, who can teach him to read and write in Braille, that sort of thing. He can't do it here on the islands. There just aren't the facilities.'

'But he can.' It was Liam's voice. 'We've been asking around. My dad says there's this lady, who's come to live on St Mary's, just retired. Dad's done some building work on her bungalow. Anyway, she's blind and she reads Braille, and she was a teacher, too, on the mainland. And so my dad rang her up and asked her if she would give Bun lessons, and she said she would. And she's very nice, he said.'

'And you know those people on St Agnes with about six children?' Dan was joining in now, 'The ones that grow all their own vegetables and have a café in the summer for the visitors, y'know, just by the lighthouse? Well, they teach their kids at home, and they're all right, aren't they? I mean, they can read and write and they can play football and stuff, just like we can.'

'And so we all thought,' Anna again, growing in confidence now, 'we thought, didn't we, that you could teach Bun here at home, and then he could go off to St Mary's for his Braille lessons with that lady, and that way he wouldn't have to leave us. So we've brought you a petition. Everyone's signed it, everyone we could find anyway, because we all want to keep Bun here on Bryher where he belongs.'

For some time no one spoke. I could hear my mother or my father leafing through what I supposed to be the petition. Then one of them got up suddenly and went out of the room. It sounded like my mother's footsteps.

'Well, Bun,' said my father, 'it seems your friends don't want you to go any more than we do. Your mum's a bit upset, Bun. Not *upset* upset, not cross, nothing like that. I think she's just touched by the nice things they wrote in this petition. I'll read it, shall I?'

We the undersigned, want Bun to stay here on Bryher with us and not go away to school on the mainland. He's grown up here with us. He belongs here. He's one of us, one of the Bryher family, and we don't want to lose him.

'And then everyone's signed it, and there's nice messages, too. Mrs Gee at the shop says, "Don't you dare send Bun away. I'd miss his mucky fingers." And here's another - old Percy at the Boathouse: "We'll be his eyes for him. Let him stay." And there's pictures, too, from some of the kids of dolphins, puffins - and an elephant. Don't know what that's doing there. He's got five feet!'

He paused for some moments. 'Of course I'll have to speak to Bun's mum,' he went on, 'and I can't promise anything. But I reckon if this lady on St Mary's is all you say she is and if she's willing to do it, then we'll give it a go. Lord knows what we'll be like as teachers. To be honest, it's not something we'd even thought of. We've got a lot of hard thinking to do, all three of us, and a lot of talking, too. We'll try to keep him with us, I promise. We'll do our best. You can be sure of that.'

CHAPTER 7

'BE HAPPY. DON'T WORRY.'

SO THANKS TO ANNA'S PETITION, I STAYED home. Three times a week, weather permitting, I went over to St Mary's for my Braille lessons with Mrs Parsons. My father did less of the fishing and was back to working on the farm most of the time, so that my mother could become my full-time teacher. I didn't learn my Braille as quickly with Mrs Parsons as I should have done, because I was reluctant to do my homework each day, and because I found it so hard to concentrate on touch.

In time, Mrs Parsons taught me a great deal more than just Braille. She taught me to be more positive, to accept my blindness for what it was; not to embrace it exactly, but to stop feeling so angry about it all the time. She herself had been blind for most of her life, after some illness or other. She'd brought up two children, travelled half the world, and been an English teacher in a school in Manchester. All with no eyes.

'I look at it this way,' she'd say (and she'd say it often – Mrs Parsons did repeat herself a lot), 'everyone out there, except you and me, has got five senses. We've got four. But it's what you do with them that counts, Bun. I'm telling you, we can see a whole lot better than they can. With our ears, we can see sounds. They can't. We can see with our noses, with our tongues, with our fingers. They can't. We make up the pictures in our head as we go along, don't we? We don't *need* eyes.'

She had a favourite little ditty she'd warble at me all too frequently, just to remind me to cheer up. It began, 'Be happy. Don't worry.' And what's more, she made the best lemon drizzle cake I'd ever tasted.

Back at home, with the help of the teachers at school, my mother had worked out a whole programme of lessons based on tapes and radio. For project work she used the Internet, too, which she'd read off for me. And sometimes, for special occasions like sports days and plays and concerts, I'd go across in the boat with Liam and Dan and the others for a day at school on Tresco, and it would feel just like old times again.

My mother wasn't a natural teacher, but she was no worse than some I'd had. From time to time she'd get a bit snappy with me, particularly when we were doing maths. We'd have a go at each other, which would end in one or both of us having a good long sulk. But then we would be friends again, after a while.

When it came to writing, though, she was inspired. 'You used to love writing stories at school,' she told me one day. 'You could do it again. Use your memory to see. Use your mind's eye. Then when you write you'll be able to see as well as anybody. You can dictate and I'll write it down.' We'd do that together often. And she was right – I found I could see my stories in my mind's eye as I told them, and that was brilliant.

My father, on Mrs Parsons' advice, to build my confidence I think, took me out with him on the farm in the tractor whenever he could. So I'd spend about half a day at my lessons in the kitchen with my mother, and then after lunch I'd be off around the farm with my father. To start with I wasn't a lot of use, of course. But after a while I began to mix the pig food for him, clean out a shed, feed the hens, collect the eggs, take the vegetables to the stall outside the house, collect the money the visitors left in the kitty. The more I did, the more useful I could be, the better I began to feel about myself, about everything.

Weekends were best, because on Friday night Anna would come home from school on St Mary's. Together we'd go on long walks right round the island, from Samson Hill to Rushy Bay, past Gweal Hill and Popplestones, up around Hell Bay, and back over the heather, through the bracken past Hangman's Rock to Fraggle Rock Café, where we'd stop for a Coke, and then home along the beach to Green Bay. She'd be my eyes, giving me a running commentary on what she saw, the birds, the boats, the people. Sometimes I'd hear an oystercatcher or a kestrel or a plover before she saw it and I'd point it out to her. I liked that.

Often, at low tide, we'd visit the stone my head had hit (now known as 'Bun's Stone' by everyone the island) and I'd jump up and down on it telling it just what I thought of it. And she'd laugh. How I loved to hear her laugh. For me these were the most magical hours of my week. We were often silent together, but it was a golden silence, a golden time.

But I hadn't dared tell her about my intermittent lapses of memory. The trouble was that I didn't know how much of my life was missing. Whenever I discovered something new, that I should have known about but had forgotten, I worried all the more. There were whole episodes I simply could not piece together. I'd lie awake at night wracking my brain to recall anything about the visit to London, or maybe the trip to Canada, but my memory remained obstinately unreliable, full of blind alleys that led me absolutely nowhere.

There was something else, too, that was keeping me awake at nights. We had money problems. Because my father couldn't go fishing as much as before, there was less money coming in from the lobsters and crabs. To make matters worse, the field of potatoes had failed – most of them had just rotted in the ground. I knew my lessons with Mrs Parsons were costing money, more money than they had. I'd hear them worrying over it and arguing about it downstairs, and of course I realised full well that I was the main cause of the trouble. They were cheery enough about everything in front of me, but all the same I could tell how tired and jaded they had become.

My father had always been a loud and laughing man, full of energy and high spirits, but he had changed noticeably in just a few months. He was having to work much longer hours than before, trying to do two jobs at once and he was exhausted. In the evenings he often fell asleep in his chair in front of the television, and he'd never done that before. When I was out working with him, he wasn't nearly as jokey and chatty as he had been. Sometimes I could feel he wanted to be alone, that I'd just be a nuisance to him out on the farm. Then I'd stay behind and listen to the audio tapes Anna had lent me and try to lose myself in a story.

Arthur, High King of Britain was my favourite. It was about a boy living on the Scilly Isles who finds King Arthur still alive and living with his dog in a cave under the Eastern Isles. The old king tells him all about his life, about the Knights of the Round Table. I listened to it over and over again, until I knew it by heart almost. Somehow, it all seemed so real to me, as if it had actually happened to me, as if I was the boy in the story, as if it was not a story at all.

CHAPTER 8

'BE AN ANGEL, BUN'

ONE AFTERNOON I WAS LYING ON MY BED listening once again to the story of Sir Gawain and the Green Knight, when my mother came in. 'Bun, dear,' she said, 'could you be an angel and pop out and fetch your father in for his tea? He's ploughing down in the potato field, I think. Can you find your way?' I didn't want to go. I hated being an angel - I wished she wouldn't say that - and was happy doing what I was doing.

'Do I have to?' I grumbled.

She said, 'Bundle!' in the way that she does. So I went.

I needed my boathook, of course, but by now I could

find my way easily enough round the farm. I knew every gate, every escallonia hedge, every rut in the farm tracks. I knew from their songs where the thrush nested, and the blackbird, too. I had the whole farm and its sounds and smells etched in minute detail in my mind. I needed the boathook only as hazard detector in case of any unexpected obstacles left lying around or blocking my path, like a bucket, or a fork, or even the tractor.

I'd walked into the tractor once before and given myself a nasty shock, and a nasty lump on my forehead, too. At least today I knew the tractor was out of the way; I could hear it chuntering up and down in the potato field under Samson Hill. So I walked on, confidently waving and tapping my boathook in front of me, and lifting my feet up to avoid tripping over the stones. There was a wind whispering in the escallonia hedges, and as I came closer I could smell the turned earth, metallic and new.

I remember I was finding the furrows of the ploughed field very unpredictable and difficult to negotiate as I staggered on towards the sound of the tractor. I kept waving the boathook and calling out to my father. Suddenly, I felt the ground open up beneath me. I dropped like a stone, feet first, grasping at something to save myself. There was nothing. I landed with a jolt and fell on to my hands and knees. Clearly I hadn't fallen all that far, because I was unhurt. I was shocked, and I was terrified, but that was all.

I felt all around me. On every side there were earth walls. In a panic, I got to my feet. There was an earth roof above me, too. I felt above my head for the hole I must have fallen through and was very relieved to find it. I had begun to imagine I might be completely entombed. I tried again and again to haul myself up through the hole, but the soil roof kept giving way and falling in on me. I must have been aware of the rumble of the tractor, but only now did I realise that it was close and coming closer, that it was heading straight towards me.

I thought my father must surely have seen me fall in, or perhaps he had spotted me struggling to get out, and was coming to help me. But then why was he not slowing down? Why was he not stopping? I screamed. I waved. But he kept coming on, the engine still at full throttle, roaring, thundering. Closer. Closer. Nearer. Nearer.

CHAPTER 9

DRY BONES

I YELLED. I WAVED. BUT IT WAS NO USE. I LEFT IT as long as I dared. At the very last moment, I ducked down into the hole and threw myself on the ground, curling up tight and screaming in my terror. The tractor was almost on top of me when the engine finally slowed and died. I heard my father calling me and scrambled to my feet. I reached for the hole above me, found it, and stuck my head out.

'Bun? Ruddy hell, Bun,' said my father. 'How the blazes did you get yourself in there?' He grasped my outstretched arms, hauled me out and dumped me unceremoniously on my knees in the dirt. Then, for some reason I couldn't understand, he began laughing, and went on laughing.

'What is it?' I asked.

'You,' he replied. 'You should see yourself. You look like a chimney sweep.' Still laughing, he wiped the dirt off my face; and then I was laughing too, out of relief, sheer relief, and because I could visualise now what I must look like. When he'd cleaned me up and we'd stopped laughing, my father turned his attention to the hole.

'An old field drain, I shouldn't wonder,' he said. 'Cracked, broken. It happens sometimes. The water leaks out and washes out its own little pool underground. A little pool becomes a big pool. Then the pool dries up and you've got a sort of underground cave. I'll have a look. You stay where you are.'

When he next spoke, his voice sounded far away and hollow. I guessed he must be peering down into the hole – I'd become good at that kind of guessing. 'Pitch black. Can't see a ruddy thing. I'll fetch a torch and have a look later. Come on.' He got me to my feet, helped me up on to the tractor beside him and we drove back home.

My mother wouldn't let me in the house. She stood me in the porch and peeled off my clothes there and then. After that it was straight upstairs and into a hot bath. 'It's everywhere,' she complained. 'In your hair, in your ears, in your nose, down your neck, everywhere.' She washed my hair for me and grumbled on and on - only half jokingly - about how accident prone I was.

'What is it with you, Bun? You dive onto rocks instead of into water. You dive down holes that were never there? What next? Haven't I got enough grey hairs? Dad says he only just saw you in time. A few more feet, he said, and he'd have driven right over you.'

Later, downstairs in the kitchen, she was rubbing my hair dry and still worrying on about what might have happened, when I heard my father come back up the path. He didn't pause outside the door to stamp his feet in the porch as he always did. Instead, he came bursting straight into the room.

'It's not a cracked drain. It's not a drain at all.' He was breathless with excitement. 'You know what it is? It's a tomb, some sort of grave. I shone the torch in. I'm telling you, it's a grave.'

I was suddenly sick to my stomach. I'd been in a *grave*! I'd laid down in a grave! Only now did I recall that it hadn't been soft underneath me, that it had felt like sticks and stones. But it hadn't been sticks and stones at all. It had been bones, dry bones! A cold shudder came over me.

'And what's more, there's other things down there, too,' my father went on.

'Don't,' my mother cried, echoing precisely my own thoughts. 'I don't want to know. I don't want to hear it.'

My father went on anyway. 'No, no, you don't understand. Not bodies, not bones. Not that sort of grave. It's a tomb, an ancient tomb, like those old tombs up on Samson Hill. You know, where they buried those ancient chieftains, fifteen, sixteen hundred years ago. So far as I know, they were always empty when they were discovered. Someone had been there before and robbed them. But this one isn't empty. There's stuff down there, all sorts of stuff.'

'What do you mean, stuff?' asked my mother.

'Well, I can't be sure, not till I've had a proper look, but there's a sword down there for a start, and what looks like a shield, too. Honestly, I'm not kidding.'

'No *actual* body?' I said still horrified, yet fascinated, too, by the more gruesome side of the discovery.

'Not that I could see. Gone to dust, I shouldn't wonder. After all, whoever he is, he must have been down there a very long time. Dust to dust, and all that.'

I had been covered in that dust, I thought, and shuddered all over again.

'I mean this could be important,' my father went on, 'this could be a really important archaeological find. And valuable, too.'

'Valuable?' my mother said. 'What do you mean, valuable?'

'Well, there could be gold down there, jewels, all sorts, you never know. You remember that Saxon bracelet a visitor found on the beach at St Martin's a while back? It fetched a small fortune up in London, didn't it? These things are valuable.'

'Not to us they're not,' my mother replied. 'If I remember our lease rightly, and I know I do, then anything that's found on the farm doesn't belong to us at all. It's not finders keepers on this place. It all belongs to the Duchy of Cornwall, to the landlord. It's in the lease.'

'Okay, so maybe you're right,' my father said. 'But it's still valuable, isn't it? And it's on our place, our farm, right? We found it. Well, it was Bun that found it, and me that did the ploughing that helped him find it – comes to the same thing. Anyway, it's ours, for the moment at least, and so we're going to get a first look at it.'

'Well if you ask me, I think you should leave it where it is,' my mother said, pouring the tea as if nothing at all had happened. 'I mean, you don't want to go digging around down there disturbing everything. It's like grave robbing. And, anyway, you're not supposed to. There's proper experts, archaeological people who know all about these things. You should leave well alone.'

By now I was beginning to worry less about the bones and the dust. I was thinking about what my father had said, that the grave was about fifteen or sixteen hundred years old. That would make it about 400 or 500 A.D. Wasn't that at about the same time as King Arthur had lived, the King Arthur on my tape?

'We wouldn't be disturbing things that much,' I said, 'not if we just took the sword and the shield. After all, like Dad said, we did find it, didn't we?'

'And besides,' my father went on, 'we can't just leave the hole like it is, can we? There's always visitors walking around. Someone could fall in and get hurt. We wouldn't want that, would we?'

My mother tried to interrupt, but he wasn't in the mood to listen to any arguments. 'Here's what I'll do.

I'll take the tractor-trailer down to the field, fetch up the sword and the shield, unhitch the trailer, leave it over the hole and then come back home. It'll take a bit of a while. And in the morning, after we've had a good long look, we can put them back where they came from. Simple. No one'll ever know the difference.'

CHAPTER 10

'ISN'T THAT MAGICAL?'

I WANTED TO GO WITH HIM BUT MY MOTHER wouldn't hear of it. She'd already lost one argument and she certainly wasn't going to lose another. 'You've got your Braille homework for Mrs Parsons,' she said firmly. 'You keep saying you're going to do it, and you still haven't done it. What's the point in paying good money for those lessons if . . .' And on, and on.

I gave in, because I knew from her tone it was a hopeless cause. I went up to my room, but I couldn't concentrate on my homework at all. I was far too wound up. All I could think about was that sword, a sword from the time of King Arthur and Lancelot and Gawain and Tristram and Percival. We had discovered it! And I would soon be holding it!

In the end I abandoned my homework altogether and put on my Arthur tape. It was the part where King Arthur is in a boat out on the lake, and a silken arm comes up out of the water offering him Excalibur, the magical sword that brought him his kingly power, the sword he would use all his life in his struggle for good against evil. I was still listening to the tape when I heard the tractor come rumbling back into the yard.

My father was already in the kitchen by the time I got downstairs, and I could hear my mother spreading newspaper out on the table, complaining bitterly.

'I'm telling you. We shouldn't be doing this,' she was saying. 'It's not right and, what's more, it's not hygienic, either.' Suddenly she stopped talking. I heard a sharp intake of breath. Then a silence. 'Oh my God! It's beautiful. Here, Bun, come and touch it.' She took my hand and guided it. 'Can you feel it?' she whispered. 'Can you feel it? It's incredible, incredible. Can you feel it? Isn't that magical?'

I ran my hands the length of the sword, from the hilt to the point. It was massive, stretching from one end of the table to the other. I had expected it to be encrusted with age, but it wasn't. It was smooth all along the length of the blade, except where it was engraved. I could feel the patterns. I found the hilt and gripped it. The moment I did so my darkness exploded into sudden light that vanished at once and left millions of fiery sparks whirling about inside my head. I tried to let go of the sword, but I couldn't. It was as if my hand was glued to the hilt, stuck fast.

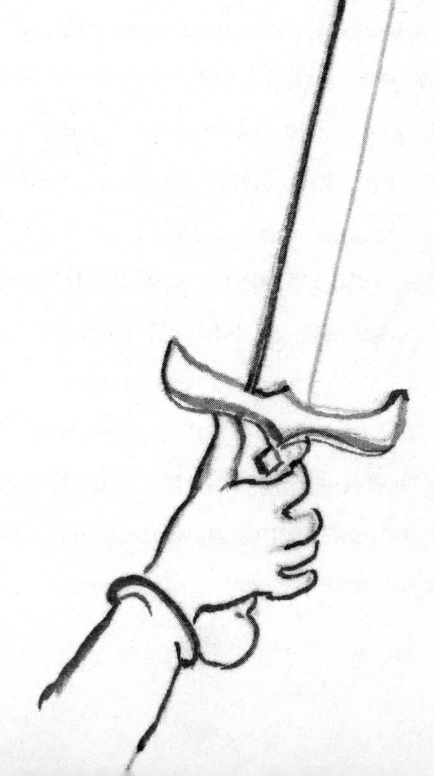

I could hear my mother's voice from far away saying, 'And to think that's been lying down there under our potatoes all these years, and it's still so well preserved. It's wonderful, just wonderful. Look at the blade. You can still see the engraving.'

My hand was suddenly released. I dropped the sword and staggered back clutching my hand. 'What's the matter, Bun? You've gone quite pale. Are you all right?' my mother asked. I couldn't answer. I felt stunned, breathless, unable to speak.

'And you just wait till you see the shield,' my father was saying. 'I'll have to unwrap it. I wrapped them both in corn sacks, Bun, so that no one could see. We don't want some nosey parker finding out about it, do we? Stand back a bit.' I heard the newspaper shifting as he laid the shield down on the table.

'Will you look at that!' said my mother. 'It's massive. How could they possibly hold a thing like that and fight at the same time? Looks like bronze if you ask me, bronze and leather. Amazing, just amazing. And there are marks on it, Bun. Cuts. Slashes. Battlescars I shouldn't wonder.'

'Here, Bun.' This time, it was my father who took my hand to guide it to the table. But I pulled my hand free of him.

'Isn't that magical?'

'What's the matter?' he asked.

'I don't want to touch it,' I said, backing away. 'I just don't want to, that's all.'

Outside in the night the Bishop Rock lighthouse sounded its horn, as if it was both warning me and beckoning me at the same time. I felt shivery all over.

CHAPTER 11

'NO SUCH THING AS LUCK'

ALL THAT EVENING I KEPT WONDERING WHAT great chieftain might have once owned the sword and the shield. What battles had he fought in? What knights had he killed? How had he died? They took photographs of the sword and the shield lying side by side on the kitchen table, then one with me in the picture standing over them, and another on the timer, all three of us together, arms round each other and laughing.

All the while I could still see sparks inside my head. I had felt an awesome power in that sword, and although it fascinated me, it frightened me more. Yet still I found myself tempted to try again, to reach out and touch it, but in the end I couldn't do it.

'I'll put them back first thing in the morning, then I'll call the archaeology people at the Duchy offices,' my father was saying. 'I expect they'll send someone at once to take them away and investigate the site. So, we'd better make the best of them while we've got them.'

All through a supper of toasted cheese and mustard sandwiches – my favourite – we talked about how extraordinary it all was, about how lucky we had been, that it had happened on *our* farm, that we had found them. Then my mother said something very strange: 'There's no such thing as luck, Bun. Everything's meant.'

And I said, 'Even my diving off the quay that day and hitting my head?'

'Yes,' she replied, 'maybe even that.'

Afterwards, my mother drew sketches of the sword and the shield just in case the film didn't come out, she said. We stayed up half the night. None of us could bring ourselves to go to bed. It was as if the sword and the shield held us in some magical thrall from which we didn't want to escape.

When at last we all trooped upstairs, leaving the sword and the shield on the kitchen table, I could not resist one last look back. Of course, I could see nothing. But quite suddenly the sparks in my head had stopped whirling, and were replaced by a pulsating glow that suffused first my head, then my whole body with a wonderful momentary warmth. I shuddered at the pleasure of it.

My mother must have felt it, for she put her arm round me to comfort me as we went upstairs. 'It's all right, Bun,' she said, 'there's nothing to be frightened of, you know.'

'I'm not frightened, Mum,' I told her. And it was true. All my fear of the sword had vanished and was replaced now by a deep longing, a need almost, to be near it again, and not just to touch it, but to take it, to hold it, to own it if only for a moment.

As I felt my way along the wall to my bedroom, running my knuckles over the familiar woodchip wallpaper, it came to me that I could, and I would, do exactly that. I would wait till they had gone to sleep, then go back downstairs and hold the sword in my hand.

'And remember, Bun,' my father went on after he'd said his goodnight, 'not a word to a soul. All we did was find them in the potato field. But we never had them in the house, right?'

I heard my mother still fretting as they went into their room. 'But I still say you shouldn't have brought them inside like that. What if anyone finds out?'

'They won't,' my father replied. 'No one saw me. Bun won't say anything, and neither will we. What do you think they are going to do? Look for fingerprints? What could possibly go wrong? Once I've put them back in the tomb in the morning, they'll just find them there, and that'll be that. The place is a mess anyway, full of stones and fallen soil. They'll never know anything different. You worry too much. Just enjoy it. Just think of it. Fifteen hundred years old maybe, and we're the very first people to see that sword after all that time.'

And sometime later I heard my mother say, 'Do you know what I wish? I wish Bun could have seen it.'

'Maybe he did,' said my father, 'in his own way, I mean. That boy's got a terrific imagination.'

'Don't know where he gets it from. Not his father's side, that's for sure,' quipped my mother.

'Thanks,' he replied, and then they were both laughing.

I lay there in bed, hearing but no longer listening to their muffled talk. The warming glow in my head was still there. Like the darkness I was so used to, I couldn't see through it, but it was so much better, so much easier to live with than that endless blackness. I knew, without a shadow of a doubt, that the glow in my head had come from the power of the sword, just as the sparks had before it.

They talked on much longer than they usually did. I knew I must wait until they were asleep, and fast asleep, too. But I was having trouble keeping awake. I kept drifting off, and then bringing myself back from the brink of sleep. I heard the Bishop Rock foghorn sounding again outside, and thought of the fog swirling in over Annet and St Agnes, rolling over the sea towards Bryher. I liked fog. It blinded every one and put me on equal terms with the rest of the world.

That was why I liked my dreaming, too. In my dreams I was like everyone else. I could see. I could see again just as I had before. The whole world of my dreams was vivid and bright and coloured, full of the faces and places I knew and loved so well. I could see oystercatchers and gannets and turnstones, and watch the Bryher gig racing down the Tresco Channel. I could see the sun setting over the sea, watch the seals basking on the Eastern Isles.

But tonight I did not want to sleep, did not want to dream. I fought back the heaviness that was coming over me. I heard the foghorn sound once more, and then there was silence. I couldn't help myself. I had to sleep. I *would go. I would go in my dreams.*

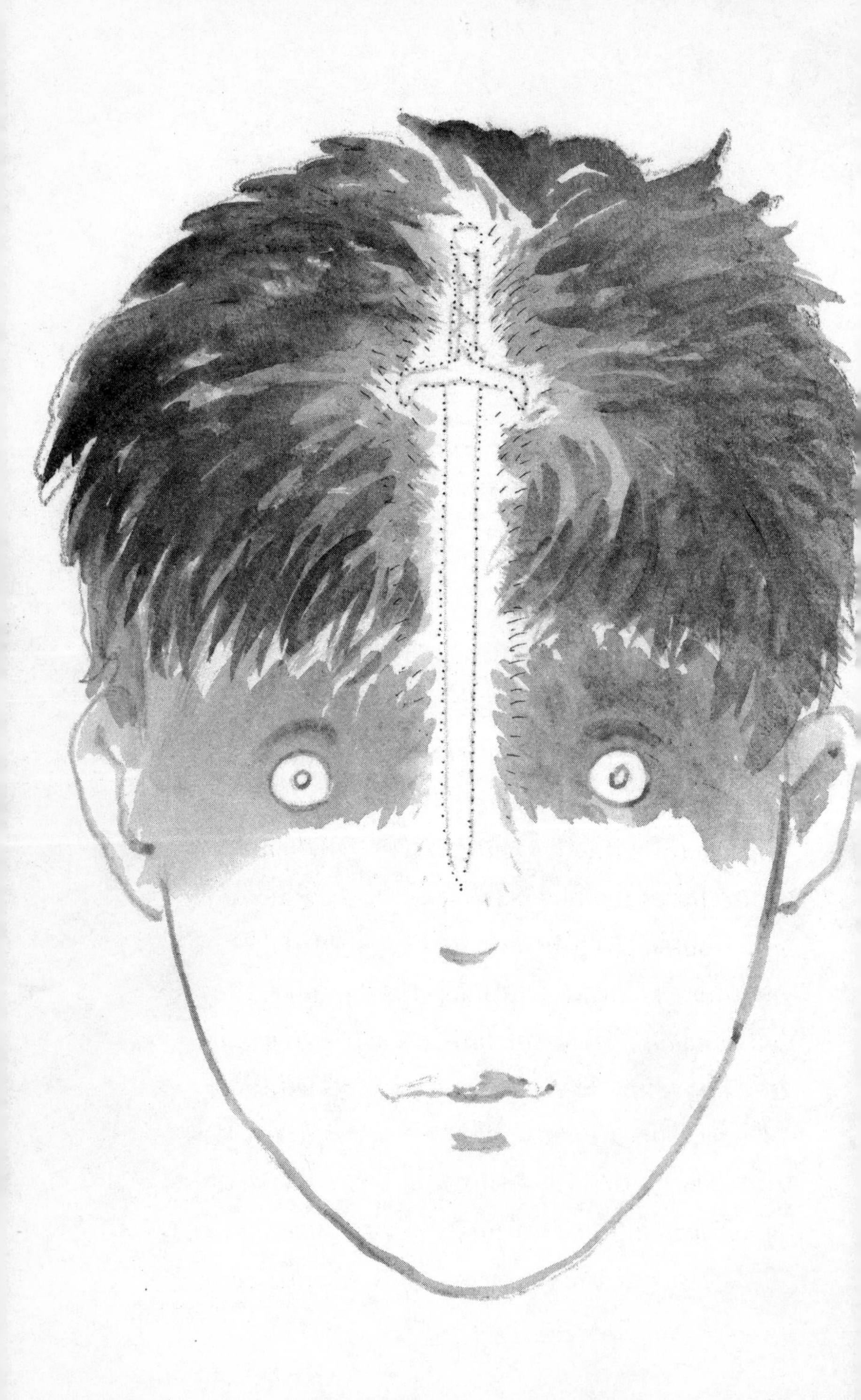

CHAPTER 12

IN MY DREAMS

THE CLOCK TICKED LOUDLY ON THE landing as I passed it by. All the way down I kept to the side of the stairs where I knew they creaked less. I lifted the latch carefully on the kitchen door and made for the table. I felt for the sword, found the hilt, took a deep breath and grasped it firmly. The glow in my head burnt bright, brighter still, then burst again, as I had half-expected it would, into dazzling light. The whole kitchen seemed to be dimly lit now, but intermittently, and I wondered how this could be until I saw through the window that the moon was full and surfing the clouds.

The sword was so heavy that I had to use both

hands just to lift it off the table. Once I was accustomed to the weight, I summoned all my strength and whirled it round my head, savouring its savage power as it sliced through the air. But I couldn't do this more than a few times before I had to lower the point of the sword on to the table and rest. That was when I had a sudden feeling I was not alone in the room. I thought at first it must be my father standing there, that I had been discovered. Then the figure moved into the moonlight.

There stood before me an ancient man swathed in a dark and tattered fleece, his long hair and beard matted with filth, his face grey with grief and age. Holding the sword out in front of me, I backed away until I felt the sink behind me and could go no further. His eyes followed me all the way, but he made no move to come after me.

'I have not come to harm you,' he said, his voice little more than a hoarse whisper, 'but only to send you on your way. My name is Bedevere from the Court of King Arthur. I have been sent by Merlin who has raised me from my long sleep, to put right at last the unforgivable wrong I did all those years ago. The sword you now hold is Excalibur. After the last dread battle I took it from the hand of the wounded Arthur, my liege king and brother-in-arms, the most noble and most unfortunate king that ever lived.

'I took his great shield also, that had so long protected our beloved Camelot. It is Merlin's wish that both be now restored to their rightful owner, to Arthur, High King of Britain. And it is Merlin's wish that this quest should be yours. You have been chosen, because you alone of living people know where to find him, where to go, for you alone have

been there. For this purpose you were sent to discover my tomb today and my poor dusty bones, and for this purpose also I have come here tonight.' His eyes filled with tears. For a moment or two he seemed unable to speak.

'I have a favour to ask of you. When you see good King Arthur, tell him that Bedevere loves him, and always did, and seeks his forgiveness. Tell him also that I did what I did, not out of greed, nor out of treachery. But I know now that in my pride I deceived my king, betrayed him, and denied his last wish. Instead of casting Excalibur into the lake, as he had demanded time and again that I should, I kept it and hid it.

'I told him only what I knew he wanted to hear, that I had cast it into the lake, that a silken arm had come up out of the water and taken the sword with it back down into the depths. And how did I know this? Because he had often foretold that at the end it would be so, that thus Excalibur had come to him and thus it would be taken from him. There wasn't a knight of the Round Table who did not know the story, how the end of Excalibur was to be.

'But I did not want to believe it was the end, that his wound was mortal, and for that reason I deceived him. I thought only to save Excalibur and his great shield, to save them for him, and so preserve the spirit of the Round Table and the holy kingdom of Camelot. All these years I have lain in my grave with my lie and longed to undo my guilt. Now at long last Merlin has done it for me and I can rest in peace. Go now. Arthur is waiting for you.'

He advanced towards me, and at once I lifted the sword to protect myself. But I had mistaken his intentions, for he simply picked up the shield and gave it to me. Then with a nod of his head, as if in farewell, he faded before my eyes.

I did not doubt a single word he had told me, for even as I stood there in the kitchen, I knew in my heart that I could find my way to Arthur, and I knew more too. I knew that in another time, in another life perhaps, I had been there. I had met him. The great king himself had spoken to me, but what he had said and where and how I had found him I could not remember.

Merlin had chosen me for this quest. He had put his trust in me, but I knew I could not do it alone. There was only one person in this world I wanted to help me on this quest, only one person I could trust.

CHAPTER 13

THE QUEST BEGINS

THE PATH OUTSIDE WAS CLEAR AND bright in the moonlight. The Bishop Rock foghorn still sounded, but I could see no sign of fog about me. I could not run, though I very much wanted to; Excalibur was far too heavy for that. I carried it in both hands, holding it out in front of me all the way, the moon glinting on its blade.

Once outside Anna's house I laid Excalibur in the long grass and ran back to fetch the shield. It didn't take long. With both sword and shield now lying in the grass at my feet, I collected a handful of pebbles from the track and tossed them up at Anna's window. I had to do it three or four times before at last I saw her face appear at her window.

She opened it and looked out. 'Bun?' she whispered. 'What are you doing, Bun? What's up? What's going on?'

'I need you,' I said. I knew that was all I had to say. Moments later she came out, pulling a coat over her dressing-gown. Without a word I gave her the shield to carry.

'I'll tell you all about it on the way,' I said, picking up Excalibur. 'Come on.'

She waited only until we were out of sight of the houses before she stopped me. 'Bun, where are we going? What are we doing?' she said. 'The sword, the shield, where did you get them? This is mad, Bun. For God's sake, it's the middle of the night.'

I told her the whole story, exactly as it had happened. She listened to me without interrupting once. When I'd finished, she simply gaped at me and said nothing at all. 'It's true,' I told her. 'All of it, I swear.'

'Are we dreaming this?' she said, looking about her. 'I mean, am I here? Is that really Excalibur? Is this really King Arthur's shield?'

'It's no dream, Anna,' I said. 'It's all as real as we are. Touch it if you like.'

She laid the shield on the ground, and I offered her Excalibur to hold. The moment she touched it I could see her eyes suddenly widen with alarm as the power of Excalibur surged through her.

'It's all right,' I said, holding it with her. 'It won't hurt you. I promise it won't.' I looked her in the eyes. 'Do you believe me now? Do you believe it's real? Do you believe it's Excalibur?'

'I believe it,' she whispered. 'I believe it.'

We walked in silence past the church and down towards the quay. 'That old man you met, the man in the kitchen, is it true what he said?' she asked.

'About what?' I said.

'Do you know where Arthur is? Do you know how to find him?'

'I only know that I will find him, and I know what will happen next. I know there'll be a galley waiting for us at the quay. It will take us wherever it will take us, wherever we need to go.'

'How can you be sure?' she said.

'All I know,' I replied, 'is that I know, but I don't know how I know.'

As we came past the graveyard the sea in Tresco Channel was moon-dappled and dancing, and there was the galley waiting for us at the quay. I put the

sword in first, leaning it carefully up against the side of the boat. Then I stepped in. After a few moments hesitation, Anna gave me the shield to hold for her, and joined me in the boat. At once the galley moved out over the sea, leaving the water quite undisturbed around us, and no trace of a wake behind us. There was no rudder, there were no oars. We were on board a ghost ship.

CHAPTER 14

GHOST SHIP

THERE ARE TIMES WHEN WHAT IS happening to you seems a distant echo of the past, nothing you could say you actually remember, but none the less you are quite sure you have been there and been through it before. As the ghostly galley glided out over the silver sea, I had exactly this sensation. I had been there before. I had done this before.

Anna and I sat silently side by side, Excalibur lying across us on our laps and the great shield lying at our feet. The Bishop Rock foghorn sounded again, and as it did so we found ourselves cocooned entirely in a sudden dense fog. We could see no rock, no island that might tell us where we were. Only the moonlight came with us, lighting the fog above us. Anna's hand crept into mine. 'I don't like this, Bun,' she whispered.

'It's all right,' I said. But even as I spoke I felt myself gripped by panic. Until that moment it was as if I had sleepwalked through all this. The truth was that I had no idea as to why it should be all right, nor any notion of where the galley might be taking us, nor what might happen to us, nor how we were going to get back. In my sudden terror I grasped the hilt of Excalibur tight, and all at once felt a great calm come over me. I knew without a shadow of doubt that we were in safe hands, that we could come to no harm.

Oystercatchers piped somewhere nearby, and I looked for them, but the fog was impenetrable. The galley sped over the sea, eastwards I thought, for the Bishop Rock foghorn sounded from behind us now, to the west, and fainter every time I heard it.

'It's not far now,' I told her, though how I knew this I did not know, and almost as I spoke we came out of the bank of fog and saw the Eastern Isles ahead of us in the shining sea. The Ganilly sandbar, lit by the moon, was a bright swathe in the ocean, *a golden arrow pointing us where we were going.*

Overhead I heard the sudden singing of wings and looked up. Six swans flew above us, their shadows moving over the water ahead of the galley as if they were guiding us in. The sea was shallow now, and translucent all around the ship, the seaweed reaching up towards us, tendrils wafting us in, waving us on, and there were silver fish flashing and flitting by, all swimming in the direction we were going. It was as if nature was taking us by the hand and leading us.

And then I knew. Then I remembered. I knew on which island we would find him. I remembered precisely where we had met before. 'Little Arthur,' I told Anna. 'He'll be waiting for us on Little Arthur.'

'How do you know?' she asked.

'I was there before,' I told her. 'I saw him there once before. I met him. I talked to him.'

The swans landed in perfect formation in the sea in front of us, drawing us in behind them towards the shore, towards Little Arthur. It was an island I knew well, that we both knew well, for it was to Little Arthur we often came for picnics in the summer. We'd lie on the top of the hill and see the seals below basking on the rocks, and watch the gannets diving into the ocean all round us.

Anna was pointing at the hilltop. 'Look!' she whispered. 'The rocks. Can't you see it? It's like a sculpture, a warrior's head. It's like he's lying there. You can see his helmet, his nose, his chin.' And it was true. The whole outline of the cliff face on the western side of the island did indeed resemble the head of a sleeping warrior, a sleeping king. The galley slowed as we neared the shore and then stopped.

CHAPER 15

METAMORPHOSIS

'THERE WERE SIX BLACK QUEENS,' I SAID, *suddenly remembering. 'When I came before there were six black queens.' And at that moment I felt Anna grasping my arm. I had no need to ask her why, for I had already seen what she had seen. A metamorphosis, a metamorphosis before our very eyes! On the shore the six swans were transformed into six black queens all in flowing black cloaks, their jewelled crowns glittering in the light of the moon, and one of them was beckoning us to come, to follow them. I climbed over the side of the galley and let myself down into the shallows. Anna leaned over and handed me down the sword and then the shield.*

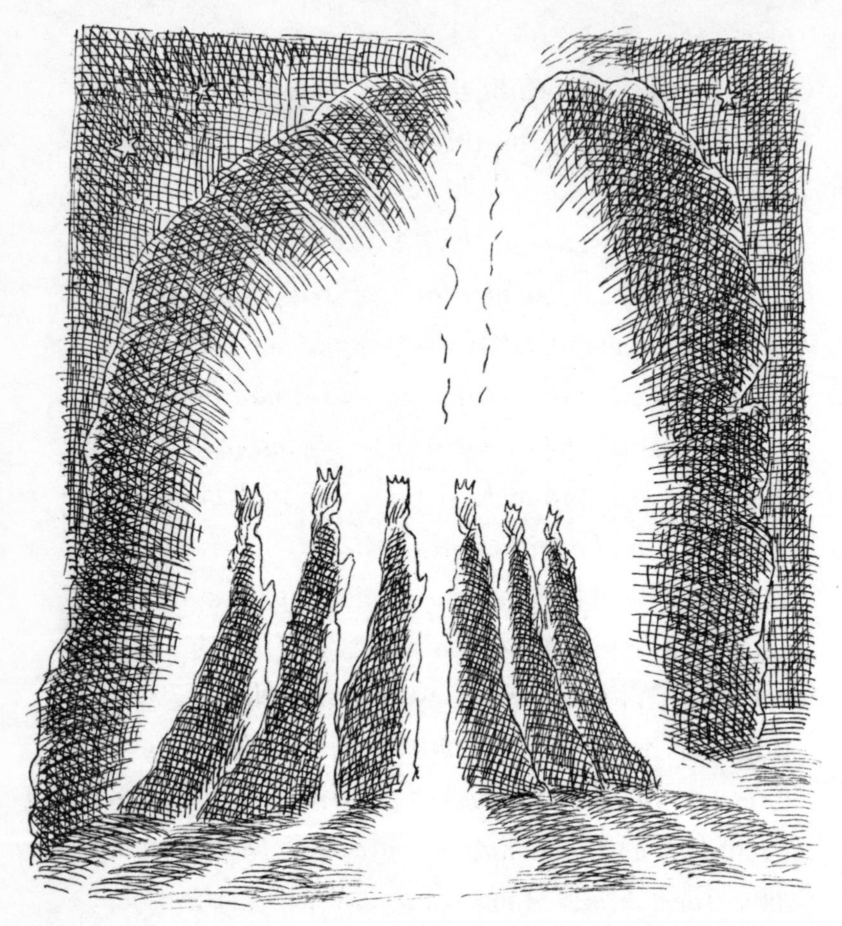

'Do I have to come any further?' she asked.

'I need you to,' I said. 'I want you to be there with me when I meet him. Please, Anna.' For a few moments she looked at the six black queens, and then up at the king's sleeping head against the sky.

'He's waiting for us,' I said. 'Please.' And then losing patience a little, I added, 'Look, I can't carry the sword and the shield on my own, can I?'

'All right,' she said, and she clambered over the side and joined me on the sand. 'I don't like them,' she whispered. 'They're like witches.'

'They're his queens,' I said. 'They look after him. They've looked after him for hundreds of years.'

It was coming back to me. I could see it all in my head now, every detail of it, just as it had happened before. As we followed the black queens up the beach towards the rocks, I turned to look back. The ghost ship had vanished altogether.

Ahead of us the rocks seemed to open up and we could see a golden glow of light. The black queens moved on in silent procession. We followed where they led into a long tunnel lit on either side by flaming torches. I was suddenly aware that Excalibur was no longer heavy to me, that it rested almost weightless in my hands, as if it was straining to leave me, longing to be back once again in the hands of the great king to whom it belonged. I gripped it tight and walked on up the tunnel, a long and winding tunnel where I now knew for sure that I had walked once before. And I knew too where it must lead us.

CHAPTER 16

ARTHUR, HIGH KING OF BRITAIN

WE CAME AT LAST OUT INTO THE VAST cavern I remembered, with its vaulted rock ceiling, and I saw the great Round Table set all about with chairs, and by the fire the dog, toasting himself with his nose in the ashes.

'Bercelet,' I whispered to Anna. 'That's his dog.' And even as I spoke the dog rose from his sleep, stretched himself awake, yawned, and came towards me wagging his tail in recognition.

From the chair by the fire came a voice. 'What is it, Bercelet? Has the boy returned as Merlin promised? Does he have it? Does he have Excalibur with him?'

The old man, who now rose slowly from the chair to stand by the fire waiting for us, was just as I remembered him, his hair and beard long and silver white, his face etched with age. The sight of him froze me to the spot, not with fear, but in awe. Before us stood the great Arthur himself, High King of Britain, the sleeping king, not dead, not a ghost, but alive, as alive as we were.

His whole life story seemed to pass before me as the king came towards us. How Merlin had called him, and trained him. How the young Arthur drew the sword from the stone in London, and became the chosen king of Britain. How he freed his people from fear and evil. How he drove out the Saxon invaders. How he loved Guinevere. How Mordred, his own son, had contrived to corrupt the kingdom and all it stood for – the protection of the weak, honour, chivalry and justice for all. How Guinevere had loved Sir Lancelot, and left Arthur alone to face Mordred at the last terrible battle at Camlan, where so many of the knights of the Round Table had perished. Where the wounded Arthur had killed Mordred, and been borne away from the beach by the six black queens in a galley, leaving Sir Bedevere on the shore.

As he came towards us, the great king was not looking at me, or at Anna. He had eyes only for Excalibur. I held it out to him, and as he took it from me, I saw his eyes close in rapture. He grasped it by the hilt, and lifted it high above his head.

'Oh, Excalibur!' he cried. 'I have you at last. With you in my hand I have the courage and the strength to be a king again, to do whatever it may be that I am called upon to do. How I have longed for this moment.' He brought the blade down and gazed into it. 'I see again reflected in this blade the king I once was and can be once more. And the next time, I shall not fail. I shall not fail myself. I shall not fail the people.'

He looked up at us and smiled. 'Merlin told me you would bring a friend with you on this quest. She has my shield, my trusty shield. Let me have it, girl, let me hold it.'

Arthur stood before us, a warrior once more, Excalibur in hand, his great shield held before him.

CHAPTER 17

THE SLEEPING SWORD

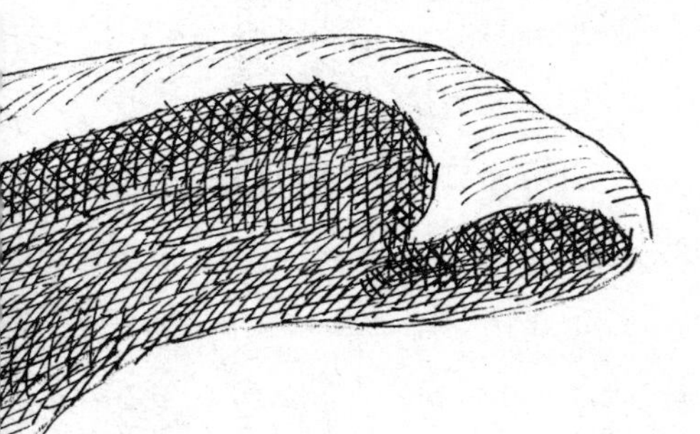

THE DOG APPROACHED THE SHIELD CAUTIOUSLY, sniffed at it once and stepped back nimbly. Arthur laughed at his timidity. 'Do you remember Bercelet, boy? Do you remember me?'

'Yes,' I replied, remembering it all now as if it were yesterday, but whether it was yesterday's truth or yesterday's dream I was not sure. 'When I was younger I was trying to walk across the seabed from island to island, and I was cut off by the tide. You saved me from drowning. You brought me back here and dried my clothes, and then you told me the story, your story.'

'So I did. So I did. And I always hoped and

believed that one day you might return,' said the great king, 'but I did not know when. And now you're here. I did not know that Merlin would choose you for this quest, that you would be the one who would at last bring me back Excalibur.'

'It was just luck, I suppose,' I told him. 'We discovered the sword and the shield at home, in our potato field. Lucky accident, that's all it was.' Arthur shook his head, turned and led us towards the fire. 'No boy. There is no such thing as luck. It was meant. All this was meant. All that happens is meant to happen. Merlin told me I should soon have my Excalibur again, that he had chosen a messenger who would bring it to me. Nothing happens unless Merlin means it to happen.'

He sat down heavily and laid Excalibur across his knees. For some moments he sat there running his hand up and down the blade, almost in disbelief it seemed.

Bercelet came to lie down between Anna and me, and looked up into her eyes. 'Bercelet trusts your friend. He loves her, and I see you do too, else you would not have brought her here. Ah, love, trust,' sighed the king, sitting back. 'To love or not to love. To trust or not to trust. This was ever the great dilemma of kings, of men and women everywhere. But I am old enough now and wise enough, I hope, to know better than I did, and I see in her eyes that she is a good friend to you and to me and can be trusted. Tell me, boy, tell me how it all happened. How did Merlin contrive to bring you to me?'

So I told him the whole story from the moment I fell down the hole in the potato field to the appearance of Sir Bedevere's ghost in our kitchen. 'He told me I had to bring Excalibur and the shield back to you, that Merlin had chosen me for the quest. And he told me other things too. He wants you to know that he loves you, and always did, and meant you no harm by disobeying you after Camlan, after the last battle. It was just that he could not bring himself to throw Excalibur into the lake as you told him. He did not want to believe you were dying, and he thought it would be the end of Camelot if he did. So he tricked you.'

Arthur laughed at this, and shook his head. 'Old men's tales,' he said. 'Old men believe what they want to believe. They invent their own myths. I should know, for I have been an old man for a very long time now. Bedevere did not trick me. My memory of that last battle is as clear as crystal. I killed Mordred. I killed my own son. No man, however old, would invent such a myth. I remember it all, every dreadful moment of it.

'After the battle, even as my queens bore me still bleeding from my wounds to the galley, I knew Bedevere might have betrayed me. He was a good man, but a weak man, too. I hoped he had done my bidding, but in truth I always doubted it. Of all my knights, Bedevere was the only one left alive. There was no one else to help me and, besides, I was too old, too tired to care, near death as I thought.'

As he talked on, as we listened, the six queens brought us each a beaker of soup and some bread, and fish laid out on a great platter. 'These I caught myself,' said the king, his eyes suddenly bright and mischievious. He leaned forward and spoke to us confidentially, almost conspiratorially.

'They let me out only from time to time, rule me with a rod of iron, and they're such silent companions. Never a word. Never a smile. No king ever had a smaller kingdom than this little isle. It is my penance. For centuries I have walked every rock of it, with none but Bercelet for company. Loyal friend though he is, he is not much of a one for conversation. But he loves a walk, to chase after the birds, and while he does so, I fish. These fish I caught early this morning. Eat my children, eat. They are fresh.'

I had not expected Anna to speak for she had done little until now but gaze at him wide-eyed. 'Excalibur, sir,' she began hesitantly, 'is it really a magical sword, as the story says?'

The great king thought for a while before he spoke. 'This sword,' he began, 'in the hands of a good king can be a force for good, for justice, for healing. But once corruption and despair have darkened and embittered the spirit, as it had mine in my later years, after Lancelot left, after my beloved Guinevere left with him, then Excalibur lost its power and became a sword like any other, an instrument of death, no more.

'And now Excalibur is but a sleeping sword, sleeping all these centuries, waiting for a new time, until his king was thought deserving of trust once again. That you have brought it back to me is a sign from Merlin that he believes I am fit once again to be king, should I ever be needed. And when that time comes, he will come himself and bid me once again draw the sword from the stone as I did before. Then, and only then, will this sleeping sword truly awaken. So Merlin has told me and so I must believe.

'In the meantime, boy,' he said, turning his gaze on me, 'when you have both eaten your fill there is one last task I have for you, that Merlin has for you, before your quest is finished. But do not hurry over your eating. It can wait. All these years I have longed to hold Excalibur again, and I do not want the moment to be over too soon.'

'How long?' Anna asked. 'I mean, how long have you been here on Little Arthur?'

He smiled at me. 'She is full of questions, your friend. And so she should be. How else do we learn wisdom? I have not counted the years, girl, but my keepers, my guardians, my six queens tell me I have been waiting here for nigh on fifteen centuries. Fifteen centuries I have waited to do this.' And the old king got to his feet, and readied himself, Excalibur held in both hands. 'And for all I know,' he said, 'I may have to wait another fifteen centuries before I can do this again. So I shall make the very best of it.'

And with that, he whirled Excalibur about his head, and cut and parried and slashed and thrust, until at last he was left leaning on the sword exhausted, his eyes bright with excitement, and laughing, laughing out loud.

Sir Galahad
Sir Lancelot
Sir Gawain

CHAPTER 18

END OF THE QUEST

THE SOUP WAS HIGHLY SPICED AND warming to the roots of my hair, to my fingertips. Both Anna and I drank it eagerly and then ate our fish in our fingers, pulling the flesh from the bones. I had never liked mackerel until then, thinking it rather tasteless – like pollock, only fit to be used as bait to catch lobsters and crabs.

When we were done eating, Arthur led us out into the centre of the great torchlit cavern, and around the Round Table, Excalibur resting easily in the crook of his arm. And as we went, Arthur spoke of all the knights whose names were inscribed on the seats, of the quests they had followed, of the wonderful feats of courage and chivalry they had each performed, of Gawain and Percival and Tristram. Even as he spoke their names, I knew their stories word for word, the stories he had told me once before.

When he came to his own seat he stopped. 'And here I sat,' he said, 'with my beloved Guinevere on my right and Lancelot on my left, and around us a company of the dearest friends, the noblest friends. Such friends, such a time.' He sighed. 'And it was all so quickly over, a tiny flame that glowed brightly, brilliantly and then flickered and faded but, thank God, was never quite extinguished, not entirely.

'When Merlin came to me in my dreams and told me I must expect you, that Excalibur was to be restored to me, I had hoped my time had come. But sadly it is not to be so, not yet. Excalibur, he told me, was to be mine again, but I may not use it, may not wield its power until he comes to see me in person to tell me the time is right. Until then I have to bide my time, and be patient, he says. And for its safe keeping Excalibur will remain here with me.

'Do you remember the sword in the stone? Do you remember how all the knights and princes in the land tried to pull it free, and that only I had the power to do it? So it will be again. Excalibur,

Merlin told me, is to be thrust into the rock you see behind you. Read what you see upon it.'

We went closer and bent down to read it. In the flickering of the torchlight it was not easy to pick out the words. I could read it only slowly.

> When the right time comes, only Arthur, the rightful High King of Britain, shall pull this sword from the stone.

'And now,' said Arthur, handing me Excalibur, 'it is for you to thrust it into the stone.' I took the sword from him and looked at the rock face in front of me. It was solid, flawless, not a crack to be seen.

'But how?' I asked. 'How can I do it? It's impossible. It won't go in.'

'Do it. Believe it will happen and it will, I promise you,' said Arthur. 'Go on. Thrust, and thrust with all your strength. Anywhere you wish. It will go in. Have faith.'

I turned and looked at Anna, and saw no flicker of doubt in her eyes. If she believed I could do it, then I could do it. I grasped the sword, and ran full tilt at the rock face, and thrust it in. The blade sunk in almost up to the hilt, as easily as if the rock had been butter.

'That was well done,' said Arthur, his hand on my shoulder. He reached for the hilt and pulled at it. 'Stuck fast,' he said. 'And so it will stay now until the day I am needed once more. You have done me great service tonight. But the night is for sleeping, for me and for you, and you must go back

home where you belong. Come.'

With Bercelet's nose touching the back of my leg as I walked, we left the great cavern behind us and went down the winding torchlit tunnel following in Arthur's footsteps. He stopped as he came out into the night air and breathed in deep. 'The air of this place is good for the body, good for the soul, too. Go now, your galley is waiting to carry you home.'

And so it was. The six black queens stood like silent sentinels on the rocks watching us go, but no one except the king himself spoke a word as the galley moved away from the shore. He waved and called out after us, 'May your days be full of laughter and light. May all our dreams come true.'

We watched him as long as we could, his great shield resting on the ground in front of him, Bercelet beside him gazing after us. Above us we heard a sudden singing – the swans, the six swans flew above, drawing us into the fog, taking us home. When we looked again Arthur was gone and the island with him.

The fog lifted as we came into Tresco Sound. All this while we had sat silent in the galley, alone with our thoughts. As we passed below Samson Hill, I looked up and saw the moon riding through the clouds, coming with us all the way. That was when Anna spoke. 'If you weren't here with me,' she said, 'I wouldn't believe any of this. I'd think it was all a dream, a wonderful dream. But I *see you.*' She put her hand on my arm. 'I *feel* you. I *hear* the oystercatchers. I *smell* the sea. It has all been real.'

The six swans flew across the moon and circled overhead as the galley came alongside the quay. We stepped off, and watched it glide away and vanish.

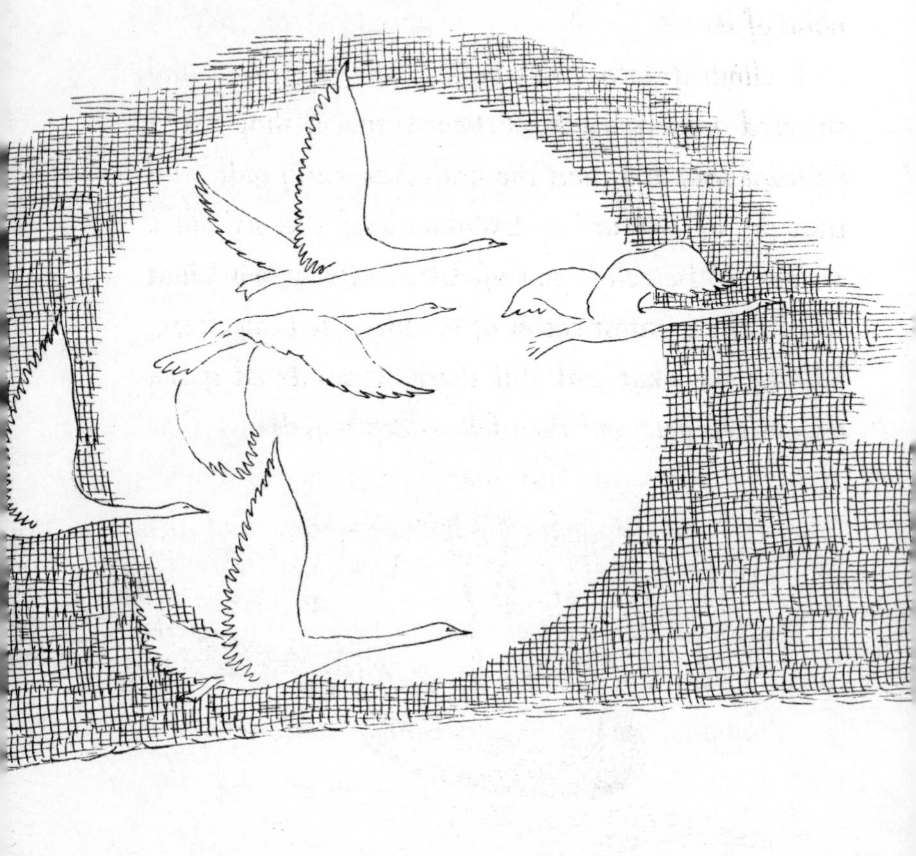

We were back on Bryher, and we were suddenly cold. We parted by the church.

'You'll tell no one?' I said.

'No one,' she said, 'It's our secret.' She kissed me on the cheek, and she was gone.

The house was still dark when I got home. Only the moon lit the windows. No one stirred. The newspapers lay spread out on the kitchen table. No sword. No shield. It had happened. I had imagined none of it.

I climbed into bed, pulled up my duvet and shivered myself warm. I heard the Bishop Rock foghorn sounding and the cry of an early gull, and thought of Arthur, of Excalibur, of the six black queens, of Bercelet, and of Anna, with whom I had shared the greatest secret of my life. I felt my cheek, felt the kiss that was still there. I wondered if she was asleep yet, and then fell asleep myself.

CHAPTER 19

'IS IT REALLY TRUE?'

I WOKE AND OPENED MY EYES. IT WAS LIGHT. It was *light*! IT WAS LIGHT? I closed my eyes and opened them again. Still light. I looked around. The Chelsea team poster I hadn't seen for two years was still on the wall, the collage of all my bird pictures was above my bed. My green dressing-gown was on the end of the bed, my audio tapes on my bedside table, and the radio too. I got up. I looked at myself in the mirror. Me. I was older, taller than I remembered, but it was me. I wasn't imagining it. I was seeing again! I could see! I could see! I could see!

I thundered down the stairs into the kitchen, shouting and screaming at the top of my voice. No one was home. The newspaper was gone from the kitchen table. I rushed out of the house, and saw them coming back up the farm track from the potato field, my father on the tractor, my mother sitting, legs dangling, on the trailer behind. I waited for them, wondering how to tell them, what to tell them.

Should I say that it was the power of Excalibur that had healed my eyes? Should I tell them everything? Should I tell them anything? As I stood there a robin sang at me from the apple tree. I remembered a robin singing at me at London Zoo, and the massive dinosaurs at the Natural History Museum. I remembered everything about the trip to Canada too, the Niagara Falls, the Toronto Tower, the black bear we had seen in the forest. I didn't just have my sight back, but my memory too.

They jumped down and came towards me. 'All done, Bun,' my father laughed, ruffling my hair. 'Buried them both, put the sword and the shield back where they belong. No one'll know a thing.'

They couldn't have! It was impossible, impossible.

'I was worried sick all night long,' my mother said. 'Never slept a wink.'

'You've put the sword back, and the shield?' I asked.

'Yes,' my father replied. 'No one'll ever know we had them out. I'll call the Duchy after breakfast.'

'But you couldn't have!' I cried. They were both looking at me in astonishment.

'Why not?' my mother asked. 'Is anything the matter, Bun?'

'No, Mum.' I was trying to work it all out, trying desperately to make some sense of it. Hadn't Anna and I taken Excalibur and the shield to King Arthur in the night? And if we had, then how could they have just buried them? But I knew it must have happened as I remembered it. Otherwise how could my eyes have been healed? How else could it have happened? I *was* seeing, wasn't I? Or was I imagining that too?

'Mum? Dad?' I said. I was bursting to tell them, but still uncomprehending, still unsure of the reality of anything.

'What, Bun?' my mother was clearly anxious about me. 'Are you feeling all right?'

'That's the thing,' I said. 'I'm feeling fine. In fact, I think I can see again. I mean, I can see you, both of you. I can see the sky! I can see the sea! I can see that robin over there on the hedge. I can see!'

They didn't take it in turns to hug me. There were four arms round me, and they were both crying, and then I was crying, and I didn't care any more about swords or shields, about what had happened or what I had dreamed. I could see and that was all that mattered.

The news was all over the island within the hour. Soon the entire house, and garden too, were full of people, laughing and crying. I'd never been so hugged in all my life. Liam didn't hug me, nor did Dan, thank goodness, but they did have tears in their eyes, and I was pleased about that.

In the end I escaped up to my room and sat on my bed, my head a whirl of incomprehensible contradictions. And that was where Anna later found me. She came over, crouched down and took my hands in hers.

'Is it true?' she said, looking up into my eyes. 'Is it really true?'

I just smiled at her.

'You can see again?' I nodded. She was the only person I really wanted to hug me, and when she did, my joy was complete.

'Anna,' I whispered, my head buried in her shoulder. 'Last night. Do you remember last night?'

'What about last night?' she replied. 'What do you mean?'

'You don't remember? You don't remember anything?' I said.

'I went to bed. I slept. That's all. What are you on about?'

'Nothing,' I said hurriedly. 'Nothing. I was just wondering that's all. I was dreaming a dream last night and you were in it, and I wondered . . . It's nothing, nothing at all.'

'You are funny,' she laughed. 'By some wonderful miracle you've got your eyesight back, and you go on about dreams. This isn't dreaming. This is real, Bun. You're seeing me, you're seeing again. It's all real.'

'I hope so,' I said. 'I hope so.'

THE END

AFTER I WROTE MY STORY

That was my very first long story, the first one I ever made up that had a beginning, a middle and an end. I didn't tell anyone about it for a long time. The trouble was that almost everyone I wanted to tell was in the story, because truth had played such a big part in it. All my characters were real people, friends, family. I hadn't even changed their names. I wasn't sure how much they'd like me writing about them.

Then one day Anna was up in my room. It was Friday evening. She'd dropped in on her way home for the weekend from school over on St Mary's. She'd got a new computer, she said, and it was brilliant. It did everything, word-processing, games, the Internet, e-mail, the lot. I came out with it before I'd even thought it through.

'I've done this story,' I told her. 'It's all on tape. I just told it on tape. I was wondering, could you put it through your word-processor? Then if you think it's good enough, maybe I could send it off to a publisher or something.'

'Course,' she said. 'I need the practice.'

She didn't come to see me all weekend after that, so we had no walk around the island as we usually did, no sitting and chatting together on Rushy Bay. I really missed it. I really missed her. On Sunday evening I was sitting on my bed feeling very lonesome and very miserable, when I heard her voice down in the kitchen. Then I heard her come running up the stairs.

'Bun,' she said from outside the door. 'Are you there, Bun?'

'What do you want?' I was deliberately sullen, angry at her for ignoring me all weekend.

'I've done it. Your story, Bun. I've done it on disk. I've got a copy. I've read it. Can I come in?'

'I suppose so,' I said, my heart beating suddenly fast. She came and sat down beside me.

'It's lovely, Bun,' she said. 'I loved it, the whole thing. It's good, and I mean good. And I liked being in it, too, being a part of it. It felt true, really true. Shall I read it to you? Would you like that?'

She read the whole thing from beginning to end without stopping. I liked her reading it, I liked the story, but most of all I liked her liking it.

Before she left I made her promise to tell no one

about it, about any of it. 'A secret,' she said, 'like our secret in *The Sleeping Sword*.' And she kissed me on the cheek. 'Like in the story,' she said, 'except this is for real.'

It was only the next day that I decided it was time I tried to venture out of the house more on my own. I was fed up with being cooped up. My mother went down to the shop after our morning lessons, and all I had to look forward to for the rest of the day was a trip to St Mary's to Mrs Parsons' Braille class that afternoon. I could hear my father's tractor rumbling away somewhere under Samson Hill. I'd go and see him, show him I could do it on my own, give him a surprise.

I went downstairs, picked up the boathook from the porch and went out into the yard, tapping from side to side. I felt my way along the escallonia hedge in the little field where we grow the daffodils, and then out over the ploughed field towards the sound of the tractor.

I was calling out, waving at my father when it happened. I felt the ground simply give beneath my feet. I went straight down landing in a crumpled heap. I was at the bottom of some kind of a hole, and the tractor was coming on towards me, closer and closer, nearer and nearer, the engine thundering, roaring, still at full throttle. I stood up, and felt for the opening above my head. I waved. I screamed. He had not seen me. The tractor was coming straight for me . . .

But suddenly I was not worried. Suddenly I knew the tractor would stop, that it had to stop. When it did, when I heard my father's voice calling me, I knew how it must be, that there would be a light at the end of my dark tunnel, and that I would reach it. It was *meant* to happen, and so it would happen, all of it, just as I had seen it before in my mind's eye, just as I had told it in *The Sleeping Sword*.

All I had to do was believe in it.

THE SLEEPING SWORD

Also by Michael Morpurgo

Arthur: High King of Britain
Escape From Shangri-La
Friend or Foe
The Ghost of Grania O'Malley
Kensuke's Kingdom
King of the Cloud Forests
Little Foxes
Long Way Home
Mr Nobody's Eyes
My Friend Walter
The Nine Lives of Montezuma
The Sandman and the Turtles
Twist of Gold
Waiting for Anya
The War of Jenkins' Ear
War Horse
The White Horse of Zennor
Why the Whales Came
The Wreck of the Zanzibar

For younger readers

Jo-Jo the Melon Donkey
Conker
The Marble Crusher
Colly's Barn
Snakes and Ladders
Mairi's Mermaid

Edited by Michael Morpurgo

Muck and Magic: Stories from the Countryside
More Muck and Magic